Get **Reading!** B

The Project

Boston, Massachusetts

SCIENCE

It's the first day of **career and technology class** after a school break. Hamid, Maria, and Karl are students in the class. They really like **career-tech class** because they often get to do interesting things. Their teacher, Ms. Cruz, always thinks of ways to make the class fun!

"Good morning, everyone," says Ms. Cruz. "It's nice to see you."

"Good morning," the students answer.

"Today we start a big project," explains Ms. Cruz. "You'll work in three teams. Who wants to be **team leader**?" asks Ms. Cruz.

Hamid, Maria, and Karl quickly put up their hands.

"Good," says Ms. Cruz. "So, you three will be team leaders. Now, each team is going to make a boat. You have one month. Then, we race on the river. The fastest boat wins!"

"What materials can we use?" asks Karl.

"We'll be using things from the **trash**," explains Ms. Cruz.

The students look around the room. There are several groups of different **materials**.

"The materials all have different **properties**," says Ms. Cruz. "There's plastic, wood, and old **steel**. There are also some old cotton clothes and **canvas** for you to use."

"Can we use **tools**, too?" asks Karl.

"Yes," says Ms. Cruz. " You can use scissors to cut things. But be careful because they can cut you, too! You can also use **glue** and **ropes**. And **hammers** and **nails**, of course."

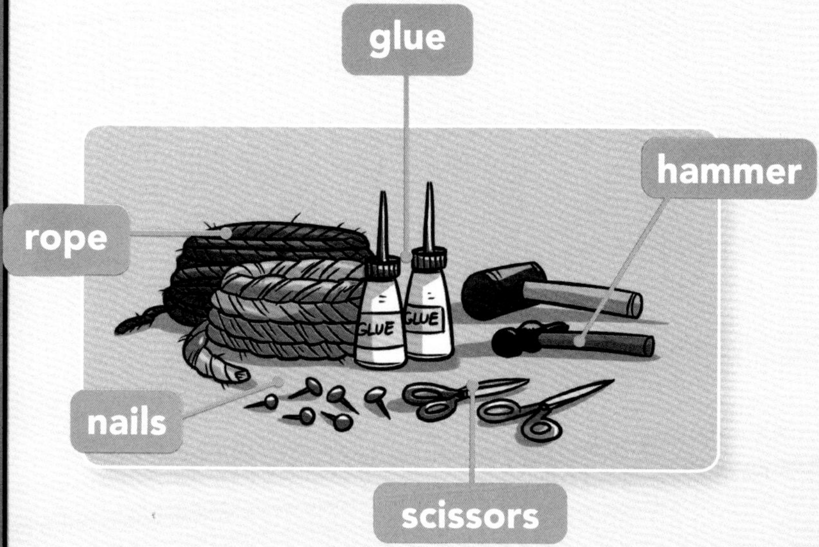
glue
hammer
rope
GLUE
GLUE
nails
scissors

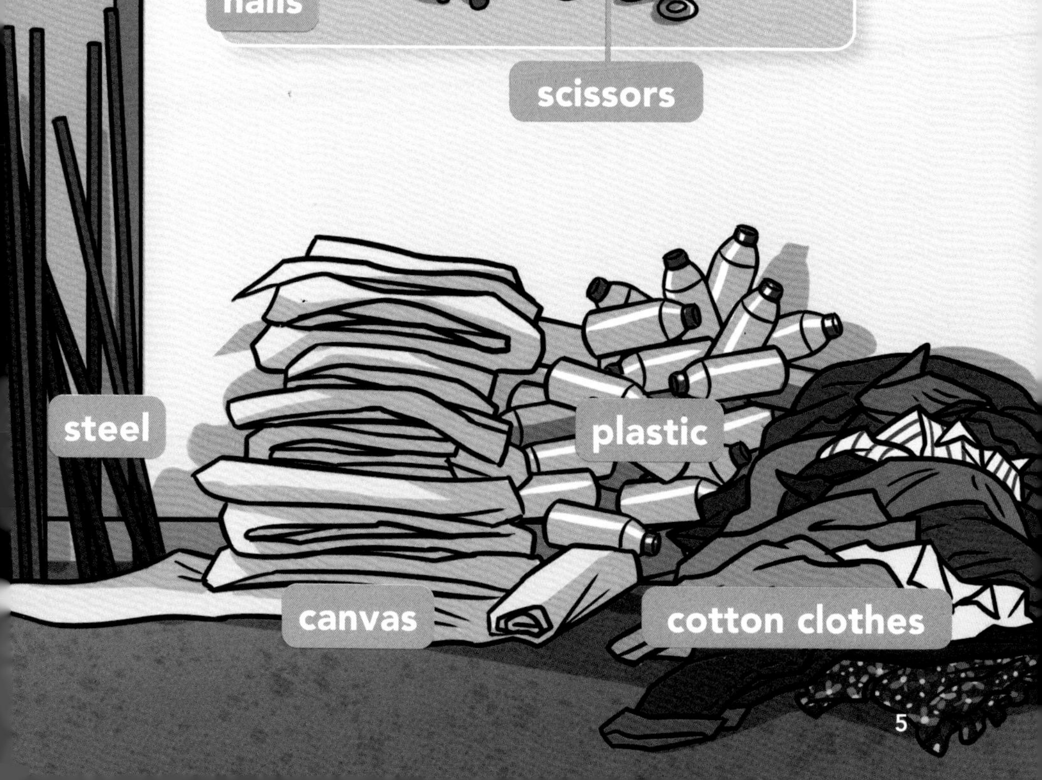
steel
plastic
canvas
cotton clothes

The teams discuss the materials they want to use for their boats. "Let's use steel," says Hamid. "Steel is strong and boats need to be strong. We can also use canvas. It's **flexible**, and it's light, too. We can put it around the steel."

"Let's use wood," Maria tells her team. "It's hard and strong. Lots of boats are made of wood." The team agrees.

"We can use plastic," Karl says to his team. "These plastic bottles are strong and flexible. We can tie them together with rope to make our boat."

Karl takes a cotton shirt. "And maybe we can do something with this cotton. It's really light, and it's beautiful too. Hmm . . ."

"Sure," says Ms. Cruz. "You can do anything with cotton."

KNOW IT ALL

Cotton is a very useful material. It's used in thousands of important products like clothes, sheets, towels, and even spacesuits!

It's one week later. Ms. Cruz is talking to the teams about their boats. "So, what's your plan, Hamid?" she asks.

"Our boat is made of steel. We're going to cover the steel with canvas," says Hamid.

"That's a good plan," says Ms. Cruz, with a smile. She goes to the next team.

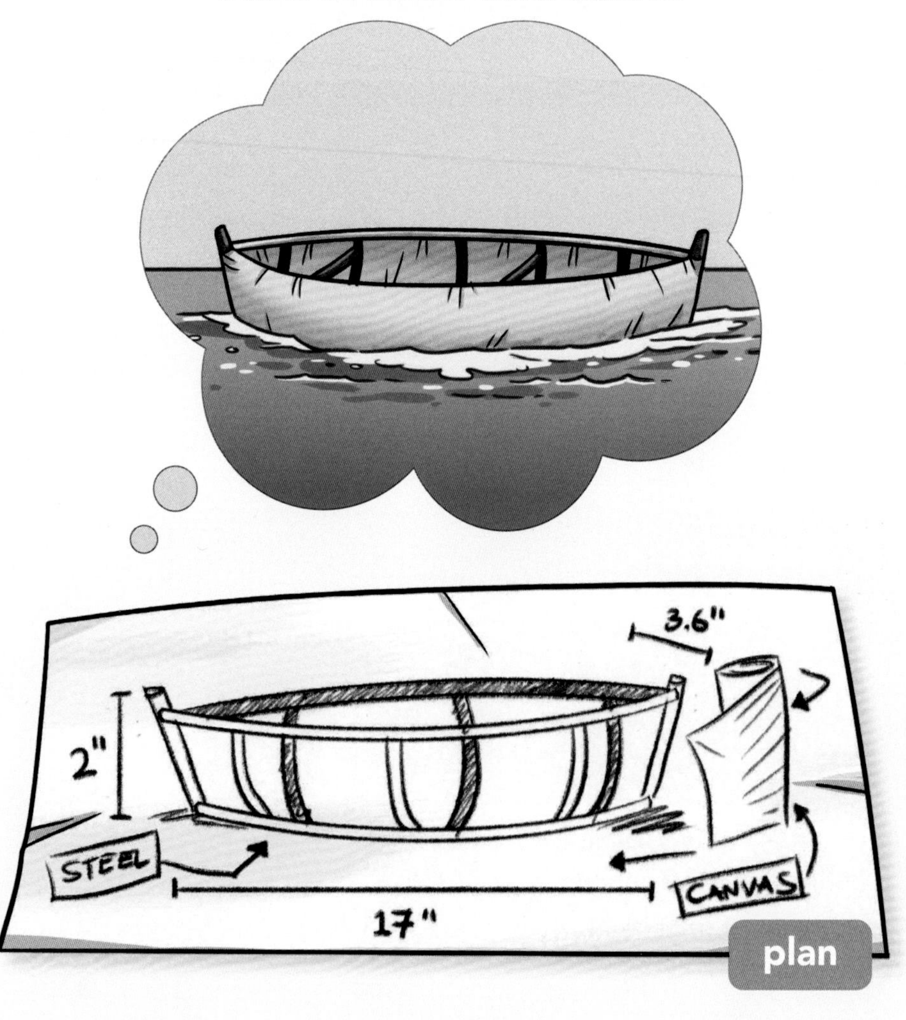

"What's your plan, Maria?" Ms. Cruz asks.

"Here's the plan for our boat," says Maria. "It's made of wood, and we're using nails and glue to hold it together."

"Good," says Ms. Cruz.

Ms. Cruz turns to Karl and says, "And you, Karl?"

"We're tying plastic bottles together with rope to make our boat," says Karl.

"Great idea. And the cotton?" Ms. Cruz asks.

Karl smiles. "Oh, that's for a new idea we're thinking about."

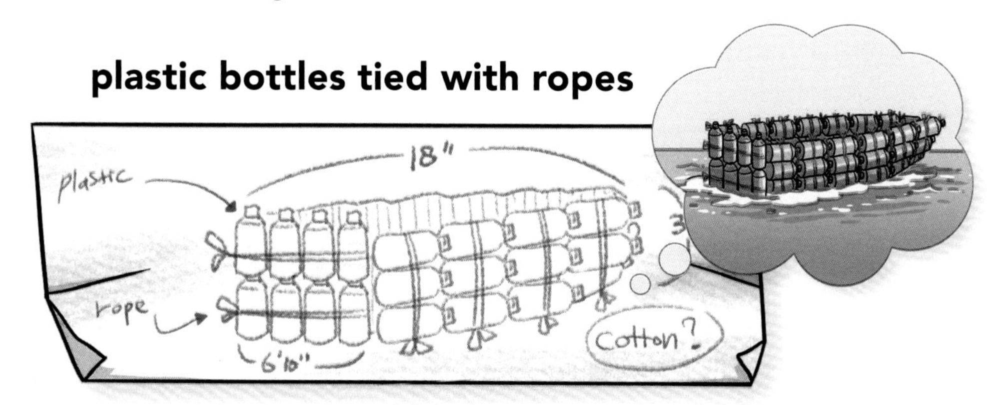

The teams work very hard, but they really enjoy the project. Soon, three weeks have passed and the boats are ready. The students take them to the river. It's a beautiful day and the students are excited. Everyone hopes that their team will be the winner. At last, it's time for the race to start. "OK," says Ms. Cruz. "Hamid's team is first."

First, the students put on life vests. Then, Hamid's team carefully puts their steel and canvas boat in the river and gets in. They start to cross the river. One second, two seconds, three seconds. "Oh, no!" says Hamid. The steel is too heavy. The boat **sinks**, and Hamid's team falls in the river!

"Oh, too bad, Hamid!" says Ms. Cruz. "OK, Maria. Your turn. Good luck!"

Maria's team puts their boat in the river. They get in and start to push their boat across. Four seconds, five seconds, six seconds.

"Oh, no!" cries Maria as water starts coming into the boat. "We're sinking!" A few seconds later, Maria and her team are in the river.

"Sorry, Maria," says Ms. Cruz. " Right. Your turn, Karl. I hope you can make it across!"

"Thanks," says Karl. He and his team put their boat in the river. Then Karl pulls some things out of his bag and gives them to his teammates. Crazy hats! They're made from cotton clothing and look really funny. Everyone starts to laugh as the team begins to cross.

Ms. Cruz watches the team and counts. Eight seconds, nine seconds, ten seconds. Karl's team is doing well, and the boat isn't sinking! Just a few more seconds and Karl's team makes it to the other side. They are the winners!

Everyone smiles as Ms. Cruz walks up to Karl's team. "Well done!" she says. "But I have one question. Why the hats?"

"Well," says Karl. "They're our lucky hats."

"Lucky hats?" says Ms. Cruz. "I haven't heard of lucky hats before."

"Yes," says Karl, with a big smile. "I got the idea from you. You said, 'You can do anything with cotton!' So we did!"

"Hmm," says Ms. Cruz. "Maybe it *was* the hats. But I *really* think it was a good team with a great design! Nice work everyone!"

career and technical education class / career-tech class a school class that prepares students for work

team leader a person who controls or takes care of a group of people working together

trash things that are no longer wanted or used

material a basic item, such as cotton or wood, that can be used to make other things

property a special quality or characteristic that allows something to be used in a special way

steel a very strong metal made mostly from iron (Fe) and carbon (C)

canvas a very strong type of cloth used for tents, bags, etc.

tool an object you can use to make things or do a job

glue something sticky usually used to join two or more things together

rope a very thick and strong piece of twisted thread

hammer a tool used to hit things several times to put them into something or change the shape of something

nail a sharp, pointed metal object usually used to join two or more things together

flexible easy to bend or change the shape of

sink to go down in something that is liquid or soft and not come back up again